MISS BUNSEN'S SCHOOL FOR BRILLIANT GIRLS

If the Hat Fits

MISS BUNSEN'S SCHOOL FOR BRILLIANT GIRLS

If the Hat Fits

Erica-Jane Waters

Albert Whitman & Company
Chicago, Illinois

Library of Congress Cataloging-in-Publication data
is on file with the publisher.

Text and illustrations copyright © 2019 by Erica-Jane Waters
First published in the United States of America
in 2019 by Albert Whitman & Company
ISBN 978-0-8075-5157-8 (hardcover)
ISBN 978-0-8075-5156-1 (ebook)

Printed in the United States of America
10 9 8 7 6 5 4 3 2 1 LB 24 23 22 21 20 19

Design by Ellen Kokontis

For more information about Albert Whitman & Company,
visit our website at www.albertwhitman.com.

100 Years of Albert Whitman & Company
Celebrate with us in 2019!

For
Samuel Winter

Chapter 1

The dusty corridors of Miss Bunsen's School for Brilliant Girls were humming with excitement as hundreds of girls made their way to the assembly hall.

Ten-year-old Pearl Peppersmith pushed her way through the crowd alongside her two best friends, Millie and Halinka.

"This news must be big!" gushed Millie. "We never get called to assembly in the middle of the afternoon!"

"What if the school has run out of money and

has to close down?" Halinka asked. "What if we have to rally together a huge girl army to save us from being school-less?"

Their headmistress, Miss Bunsen, was famous for many things, like her invention of the Herbal-Tea-Fueled Assassin Catcher. There was nothing in the school that Miss Bunsen didn't sort out, from inventing a self-cooking, -serving, and -washing-up cafeteria to designing a school uniform made of fabric that never wore out. But this left little time for important things like paying the bills or finding the money to mend the leaky roof, and every year the girls worried that their school might finally shut down—if it didn't fall down first.

"Oh, Halinka!" Pearl said, wrapping an arm around her friend. "Let's not jump to conclusions. Maybe there are just squirrels blocking up the pipes again."

Halinka threw her arms in the air. "Curse those squirrels! Why, I should invent a squirrel-fighting robot!" She looked sideways at Pearl before acting out a robot-on-squirrel battle. "Take that, Fluffy, *pow, pow, pow!*"

"I think we should probably hurry," Millie said, ducking Halinka's punches and ushering them into the main hall. "We shouldn't keep Miss Bunsen waiting."

The ancient assembly room showed its age in the afternoon sunlight. Cobwebs dangled from the gnarled oak beams that barely supported the roof, and the tall stained glass windows were filled with wide cracks that allowed the autumn chill to blow through.

Pearl pulled her blazer closer up around her

4

neck as she and her friends made their way to the front of the room. The wooden bench creaked beneath them.

"Settle down, girls," Penelope, the head girl, bellowed. "Miss Bunsen is about to arrive."

At that, the heavy side doors that led off to the teachers' lounge swung open, and the headmistress swooped in, her tattered black cloak fluttering behind her.

"Is that a bird in her hair?" Pearl whispered, squinting.

"At least it's not a squirrel!" Millie giggled. "Remember last year?"

Pearl watched Miss Bunsen as she took the stage. Despite her crazy hair and haphazardly applied red lipstick, she had an air of dignity and intelligence about her. Everyone who knew her respected her, and the girls loved Miss Bunsen for her endless ideas and inspiration. The school was indeed in trouble, but Miss Bunsen's genius and determination had saved it so far.

"Girls!" she began, reaching out her arms and unsettling the bird nested in her hair. It flew off into the rafters, cawing bitterly. "I have some fabulous news to share with you all."

A flurry of gasps and whispers erupted around the hall.

"I have just received a letter from the world-famous inventor Professor Petrinsky."

Miss Bunsen held up a tattered scroll, tied with a red ribbon. With a flourish, she slipped off the ribbon, and the scroll unrolled dramatically. All around Pearl, the audience applauded.

"That's a letter?" Halinka asked in disbelief.

"Well, he's very old school," Millie whispered, pushing her large, round glasses back up her freckly nose. "Professor Petrinsky is quite

the genius. He is *the* most celebrated inventor of his time."

"What time was that?" Halinka whispered back. "Ancient Egypt?"

"Girls," Miss Bunsen continued. "We have been invited to take part in a very special interschool competition. The challenge is to invent the perfect gadget for the youth of today, a gadget that in some way improves the daily life of a modern child immeasurably."

A whoosh of excitement swept over the assembly hall as ideas and inventions began to pop into heads.

"But that is not all," said Miss Bunsen, trying to make herself heard over the buzz. "There is to be a grand prize!"

The hall fell silent again.

Miss Bunsen leaned in close to her podium.

"The prize is £100,000." She raised her head and seemed to look every student square in the eye.

"My brilliant girls," she said solemnly, "I'm sure you don't need me to remind you of the pickle this school is in. We have barely enough funds to last the term, and if we don't win this competition...well, I'm afraid the school will have no choice but to close for a time until repairs are made. In that case, you would all be sent to..." Miss Bunsen put a hand to her heart and looked down at her purple shoes. She took a deep breath, collecting herself. "You would all be separated and sent to other schools. Our wonderful Bunsen school family would be broken up for many months."

No one could listen anymore. Murmurs of despair filled the hall.

"We can't be split up! What would I do

without you?" Millie shrieked, clasping Pearl's and Halinka's hands. "This is the only school I ever want to go to!"

"This school is *not* going down without a fight," Halinka replied, raising her arms into squirrel battle position again.

"Don't you worry, Millie. We'll make sure we win this competition," said Pearl calmly. "Miss Bunsen's School for Brilliant Girls is too special to close, even for just a few months."

As the hall quieted, Miss Bunsen continued. "I know this is extra work on top of your assignments, but I would like every girl in this school to design an invention to be put forward. You can collaborate or work individually. I will pick the best idea to go to the

11

final competition. Unfortunately, we are on a very tight deadline: the competition is in three days' time. We would have had two weeks like all the other schools, but the squirrels ate the first letter."

Pearl laughed as Halinka muttered to herself.

"Please bring your prototype creations here to the main hall after school tomorrow. Whoever wins will have all the resources of our school at their disposal." The headmistress smiled and wiped a tear from her eye. "I know you can do it, girls. I know you can win this competition and save Miss Bunsen's School for Brilliant Girls from this predicament."

Chapter 2

The next morning, Pearl chained up her solar-powered scooter by the bike shed and glanced at the row of wonderful contraptions that had been built by her fellow Bunseners.

There was Bethany Byte's geomagnetic skateboard that could reach 25 miles per hour during a thunderstorm; Saffie Sidcott's electric bicycle, charged by battery-powered fairy lights; and, of course, the Martello triplets' hoverbed, which they used to sleep in during the commute to school.

Pearl took off her helmet as she leaned up against the rusty railings and waited for her friends to arrive. A rustle behind her brought her attention to Mr. Bell, the school caretaker, who was proudly sweeping autumn leaves from the school gatehouse steps.

"Good morning, Mr. Bell."

"Well, good morning, Miss Peppersmith. How is your fine scooter performing today?"

"All good, Mr. Bell. I'm just hoping there's enough sun today to charge it up before it's time to go home!"

Nine shrill beeps sounded from further up the hill.

"Ah, Atom Academy's first call to class. Right on time, as usual," he said, checking his watch. He looked in despair at the clock tower of Miss Bunsen's School, which still read twenty to nine. "Every time I reset it, the squirrels get to it within the hour."

"At least we get extra time for a chat." Pearl smiled at the kind old gentleman. "Atom Academy is so rigid and buttoned up. I'd rather be here any day."

"Yes, quite," Mr. Bell replied. "Atom tried to hire me many moons ago, you know, my being such a professional caretaker, you see. But I turned them down. Of course, Atom Academy has a 'self-cleaning' function. I wouldn't be happy with that; I can't be happy unless I have my dustpan and brush." Mr. Bell held up a pan full of crisp orange leaves.

"Move it, Fluffy!" came a cry from around the corner. Halinka rode in on her Tea-Powered Turbo Trike, followed closely by Millie, who was wobbling about on her Smoothie-Making Penny-Farthing. "I don't know what those squirrels have got going on today, but them hanging around in the middle of the street is not helping with my schedule!" Halinka said, removing her helmet and leather gloves.

"Here," Millie chirped. "Try a nice kale and walnut smoothie. It'll get your day off to a good, whole-some start."

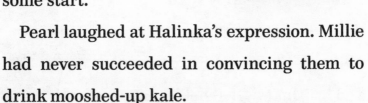

Pearl laughed at Halinka's expression. Millie had never succeeded in convincing them to drink mooshed-up kale.

"Hey, Pearl!" Pearl turned at the sound of a

familiar voice and saw her old friend from her neighborhood, Alima, walking with two other girls. Ever since Alima started at Atom Academy and Pearl at Miss Bunsen's, they hadn't run into each other around the neighborhood.

"Hey, Alima," said Pearl as she hugged her friend. "I haven't seen you in ages!"

"I know! The Atom homework schedule is very intense." Alima gestured to her companions. "These are my classmates, Megan and Heather."

Alima, Megan, and Heather looked immaculate in their Atom Academy uniform with its sky-blue dress and white shoes and socks. All three Atom girls were holding identical scooters made from shiny white plastic and aluminum.

"Those are pretty smart-looking scooters you've got there," Millie said. "What kind of smoothies do they run on? Strawberry?"

"They don't need to run on anything," Heather

scoffed. "They're just scooters that look good. We've got all the top-of-the-line materials at Atom."

"But what do they make?" asked Halinka, chewing on a toothpick. She bent over to examine a scooter, but Megan snatched it away.

"Goodness"—she laughed haughtily—"why would they need to *do* anything if they *look* this good?"

Halinka raised an eyebrow. "They're just not terribly inventive, that's all."

Heather and Megan looked sharply at each other, and then at Alima, who seemed to shrink a little. Sensing some tension, Pearl butted in. "Speaking of inventiveness, are you gals entering Professor Petrinsky's competition?"

"Oh, that charming little thing with the cute prize?" Megan and Heather rolled their eyes. "We haven't even started yet. It won't take us long to rustle some old thing up. It's just a formality, really. Atom hasn't lost a competition in, like, ever."

Alima looked embarrassed by her friends' stinky attitude. "What about you?" she asked. "Is Miss Bunsen's submitting an invention?"

"Well, they've got plenty of scrap materials to keep them busy," Megan said, laughing and pointing at Bunsen's bike shed.

Halinka bristled, and Alima said quickly, "I think your inventions are awesome. I wanted to come to Miss Bunsen's, but my parents sent me to Atom."

With a metallic clunk, a cat appeared from behind the gatehouse in pursuit of a squirrel he had failed to catch. He looked up at Pearl and batted a mechanical eye. No one knew for sure how old Miss Bunsen's cat was,

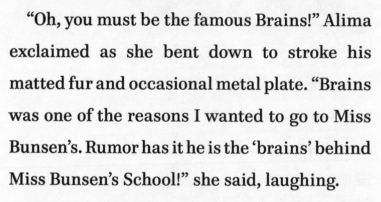

but his parts had been mostly replaced with metal plates, nuts, and bolts, and had two rickety wheels instead of back legs.

"Oh, you must be the famous Brains!" Alima exclaimed as she bent down to stroke his matted fur and occasional metal plate. "Brains was one of the reasons I wanted to go to Miss Bunsen's. Rumor has it he is the 'brains' behind Miss Bunsen's School!" she said, laughing.

Heather looked at her watch as the final call for class beeped out from Atom Academy. "Come on, Alima, you know dirty cats aggravate my allergies. Let's go."

Millie gasped, and her face went red. "It's okay, Brains," she said. "We know you can't wash up properly because of all your electronics." If Megan and Heather had dared to giggle at this,

Halinka's glare would have silenced them.

Alima had frozen with embarrassment and was still crouched beside the offending cat, so Pearl ran up to her. "It's okay," she said, hugging her again. "We'll catch up some other time."

Smiling gratefully at Pearl, Alima nodded before pushing off on her perfect scooter. The Atom girls gasped.

"Alima, what are you thinking? Don't get your scooter dirty!" Megan handed her a handkerchief to wipe down the scooter. "What will we do with you?"

And so Pearl, Halinka, and Millie watched the three Atom girls push their beautiful, identical scooters up the hill to the academy. When

Megan and Heather weren't looking, Alima glanced back with a little apologetic wave, then hurried to catch up.

"Their scooters are so perfect. *They* are so perfect," Millie said, defeated.

"Perfectly pointless!" Halinka cried. "They didn't even *make* them!"

"There's nothing those girls at Atom Academy can do that we can't. They're not going to win this time," said Pearl.

Brains meowed in agreement.

"But they have all the most recent stuff and all the latest technology," Millie replied.

"But they're not Bunsen girls, Millie," Halinka said, pointing at the dilapidated school behind her, with its missing windows and squirrel problems. "Bunsen girls live on the edge! Bunsen girls don't need all the latest ridiculousness."

"Halinka's bang on," Pearl said, putting her hand on Millie's shoulder again. "They haven't got what we've got."

"Squirrels?" Millie looked up through her wide glasses.

"Inventiveness, creativity, and determination," Pearl said gently, reciting the school motto. "The best invention will win the competition, not the shiniest. We've still got a chance."

"A chance?" Halinka cried out, becoming quite red in the face. "We are going to *win* this thing. We have to save our school. If we leave even for a few months, the squirrels might move in for good."

The school bell thudded—it had lost the

ability to ring long ago—and
several squirrels scurried out
onto the roof.

"You see, Millie? They're taking over already!"

"Come on, girls," Pearl said, throwing her tool
bag over her shoulder. "We've got an invention
to create."

Chapter 3

"Good morning, girls!" chirped Miss Bunsen as she lit a long match and slipped it inside the old, rickety boiler in the main corridor. "I've been trying to light this since seven, but the blasted thing won't fire up!"

The three friends glanced down at the large pile of matches by Miss Bunsen's feet. Brains, who had followed them in, began pawing out any that were still smoking.

"Let me have a look," Millie said, peering inside the ancient cast-iron contraption.

"Here's your problem," she said, and pulled out a used tea bag. "No wonder the school smelled like chamomile last week."

"Well, sugar my spark plugs. I wondered where I'd put that!" Miss Bunsen exclaimed with a wink. "Might even get another cup out  of this one!" She lit the boiler with a flourish and picked up Brains before clopping off down the corridor.

"I guess the usual lesson timetable is out today," said Pearl. Not that Miss Bunsen ever kept a really strict schedule.

"Well, come on then," Halinka said, marching

off. "We've got to start inventing somewhere, and I say we do it in the cafeteria! I can't work when I'm hungry."

Pearl and Millie followed her, peering into all the different classrooms full of girls frantically inventing.

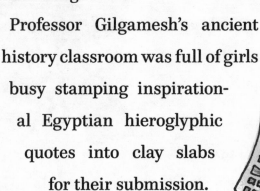

Professor Gilgamesh's ancient history classroom was full of girls busy stamping inspirational Egyptian hieroglyphic quotes into clay slabs for their submission.

Mrs. Ballast was showing some girls how to perform self-defense using medieval weaponry for a do-it-yourself self-defense kit. The chemistry

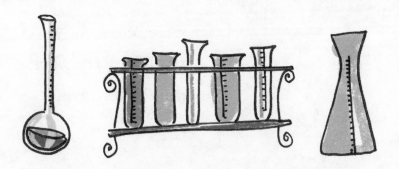

lab was the busiest classroom, with plumes of brightly colored smoke and the odd explosion filling the air.

These inventions were great, but Pearl wondered if they would truly help every kid. She and her two friends would have to do something completely different and extra special to have a chance of winning the competition.

Pearl was still thinking when they entered the cafeteria. A long conveyor belt wound its way up and down and around the room like a huge mechanical caterpillar, carrying dishes. These

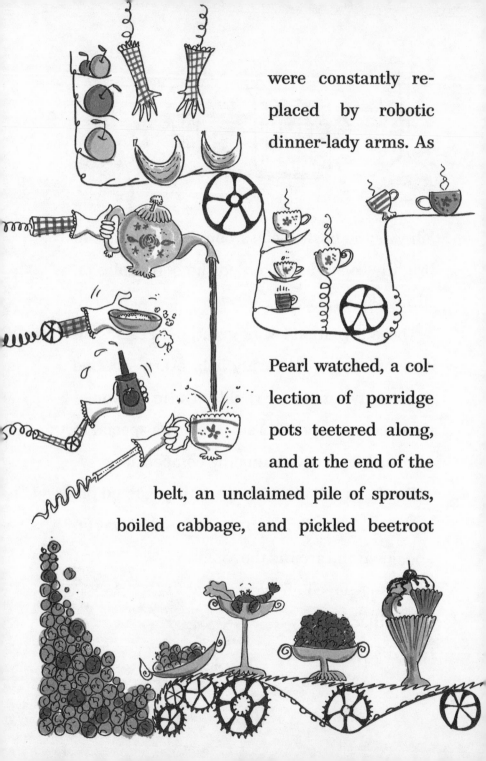

were constantly re-
placed by robotic
dinner-lady arms. As

Pearl watched, a col-
lection of porridge
pots teetered along,
and at the end of the
belt, an unclaimed pile of sprouts,
boiled cabbage, and pickled beetroot

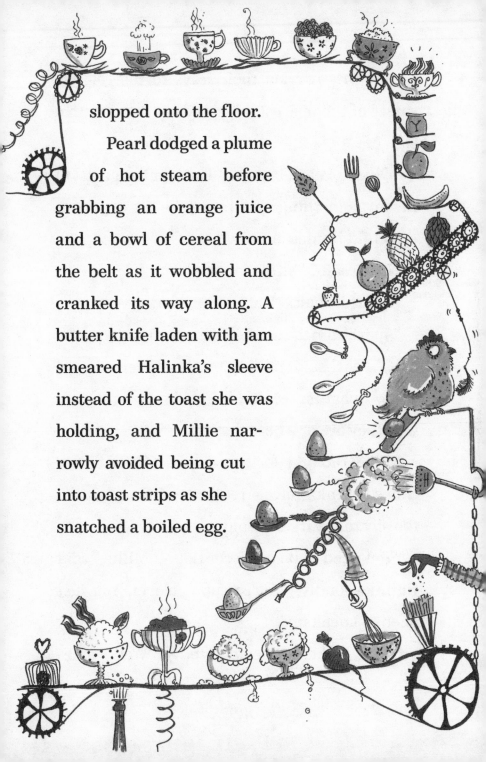

slopped onto the floor.

Pearl dodged a plume of hot steam before grabbing an orange juice and a bowl of cereal from the belt as it wobbled and cranked its way along. A butter knife laden with jam smeared Halinka's sleeve instead of the toast she was holding, and Millie narrowly avoided being cut into toast strips as she snatched a boiled egg.

The girls carried their trays to the relative safety of the nearest table and sat down with a sigh of relief.

"Okay," Pearl began. "The challenge is to invent 'something to improve the life of a modern child immeasurably.'"

"Ice cream?" Millie laughed.

"Squirrel bait?" Halinka snarled.

"Apart from the need for ice cream and squirrel bait," Pearl said, pulling out her notebook and pens, "what issues do all kids have, no matter who they are or where they live?"

Millie thought for a moment. "Well, sometimes I think I have a really good idea, but I'm too shy to say it," she said.

"You need to be more confident, Millie," said Halinka loudly. "You're super clever. You just need to speak up!"

Millie looked at her pointedly. "Well, some-

times when I do, I can't make myself heard. Everyone else just talks louder than me."

Pearl began scribbling down notes.

"I have no problem at all with talking," Halinka said, taking a slurp of tea. Millie snorted. "But sometimes I just blurt out the first words that come into my head. If I don't stop to think, sometimes I come across a bit snippy."

Halinka stared at the table, while Millie patted her arm and gave her a reassuring smile.

Pearl looked up from her notes, distracted by

a brown curl tickling her nose. "And I wish that when I tied my hair up in the morning, it would actually stay in place and leave me to focus on what's important! I get distracted too easily."

"If only there were something you could just plunk on your head that could help you be the best version of yourself," said Millie.

"Like a hat," Halinka added.

"That's it!" Pearl began furiously sketching and scribbling in her notebook, then held it up to show her friends.

"Presenting the Best of Yourself Hat!" she cried.

"The perfect accessory for the modern kid. It helps you remember those big words you need to explain something, while stopping you from blurting out the wrong thing! It gives you a sense of confidence so you know what you say will seem witty, clever, and charming, and all

the while your hair will be perfect underneath!"

"That's excellent!" said Halinka. "Can you work in some squirrel-fighting capabilities?"

"I'll see what I can do," Pearl promised. Halinka leaned across the table, and they stared at the blueprints until Millie cleared her throat beside them.

"It's a great idea," she said. "But can we build it in time?"

"We might as well try," said Pearl. "Halinka, are you done eating? Let's get to work!"

They worked long into the afternoon. Pearl drafted detailed blueprints. Halinka crafted a perfectly shaped hat that would hold all the technology while still looking properly trendy. Millie designed all the circuitry, and with a flash of her soldering iron, the hat was wired up—a little haphazardly, but it worked. By the end of the day, the prototype was complete.

They stepped back from the table and looked at their creation.

"Could it win?" Millie squeaked.

"Of course it could!" Halinka replied.

Pearl checked her watch. "We need to get it over to the main hall for judging. It can only win if it's chosen to go to the finals."

Together, they carried the Best of Yourself Hat prototype to the main hall and placed it on the judging table. It was nestled among countless remarkable inventions.

Pearl was exhausted as she cycled home but satisfied that they had done their best. Even if she didn't win, one of those prototypes had to take home the gold. They would do Miss Bunsen proud.

Chapter 4

The main hall buzzed with excitement as the entire school gathered to find out whose invention had been chosen.

The projects on display were extraordinary. The tiniest Bunseners had invented perfect pea-gathering forks and a clever spray to keep a student's socks from falling down at playtime. The middle-age girls had  found a way to make cookies and sweets healthy and had even produced a cookbook.

Pearl, Halinka, and Millie were
in the oldest group of Bunseners,
whose creations were truly special.

There was a pair of sneakers with
super-bouncy soles that could hover
two feet off the ground, and a glow-in-
the-dark geometry set that could do
a student's trigonometry homework.

There was a metal detector that
could instantly categorize and date
coins, a set of virtual reality goggles
that allowed the wearer to study
in any library the world over,
and an automatic, instant
excuse maker powered by
broken safety pins.

"Wow! Good show!" Millie said in awe.

As Miss Bunsen walked up onto the stage, adjusting her wild hairdo and clearing her throat, the chatter in the room quieted to a low murmur of "good luck" and "fingers crossed."

"My brilliant girls," she began tearily. "You have outdone yourselves. Never in all my years as headmistress of this school have I ever been so proud."

Miss Bunsen removed her glasses and frantically pressed a button on her sleeve until a handkerchief sprang out, only to poke her in the eye.

"I shall make this quick, as the winning team has much work to do. This invention has been chosen for its simple idea. It is a creation that really can help any child, no matter what age, background, or anything else. The winning invention is…the Best of Yourself Hat."

The hall burst into applause as Pearl looked at her friends, overjoyed and astonished. Halinka punched the air, and Millie teared up. Miss Bunsen cleared her throat. "Congratulations to Pearl Peppersmith, Halinka Harrison, and Millie Maranova. Girls, please come to my office immediately after the assembly."

The girls couldn't stop beaming as their schoolmates patted their backs and hugged them. But Pearl knew that their victory came with great responsibility: they had to win the competition and save Miss Bunsen's School for Brilliant Girls. Everyone was counting on them.

Edging through the cheering throng, Pearl, Halinka, and Millie made their way to Miss Bunsen's attic office.

"I've never been to Miss Bunsen's office," Halinka said. "Never, in all my years at this school."

"That surprises me," Millie said innocently. Halinka shot her a look, though Millie didn't seem to notice.

"I've never heard of anyone ever being called to Miss Bunsen's office," said Pearl, and she seemed to be right. The stairs leading to the office groaned at being put to use. "I have a feeling there is more to this competition than we thought."

They reached the office door, which was

rather less grand
than they had
expected. It was
riddled with wood-
worm, and the once-
beautiful carvings
were covered with

cobwebs. Brains was curled up outside on a
cushion. He peered at them from behind his
paws. Before they had a chance to knock, a
voice trilled faintly from within.

"Come in, do come in. Probably best not to
knock on that old thing in case it falls apart
completely!"

Inside, they found Miss Bunsen at the far end
of a long, low-ceilinged room that must have
spanned the entire length of the school. She
was looking at a blurry image on an old TV set
that showed the area outside her office door.

The girls walked slowly through the attic, tilting their heads to the side every so often to avoid the beams.

"Ah, yes, I should explain," Miss Bunsen said as the girls approached her desk. "Brains's glass eye doubles as a fabulous security camera. He keeps 'an eye' on things for me. This blasted thing is a bit unreliable though," she said, thumping the television three times and adjusting the aerial before the screen flickered to blackness. "Oh, seems to have packed up for good this time…"

The glass roof was missing several window-panes. But each empty space had a complex system of gutters that trailed from it and led to raised flower beds that overflowed with enormous pumpkins. Pearl, Halinka, and Millie stared in disbelief at the indoor pumpkin patch.

"At least when it rains, my orange beauties get

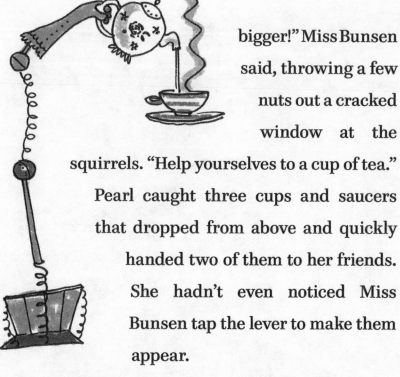

bigger!" Miss Bunsen said, throwing a few nuts out a cracked window at the squirrels. "Help yourselves to a cup of tea." Pearl caught three cups and saucers that dropped from above and quickly handed two of them to her friends. She hadn't even noticed Miss Bunsen tap the lever to make them appear.

"Mind the teapot!" Miss Bunsen chirped as a steaming pot of hot tea shot out on a mechanical arm from a trapdoor in the floor. "Now come and sit down, my little sprockets. I have some things to discuss with you."

They walked slowly to the chairs in front of Miss Bunsen's desk, trying to balance their cups of tea. Pearl wondered if her friends were as nervous as she was.

"Thank you, Miss Bunsen, for choosing our design," Pearl began. "We—"

"Nonsense! You were the clear winners." She smiled at them across the desk. "There is something very special about you three, especially when you work as a team. I've seen many geniuses pass through these corridors over the past one hundr—I mean, the past few years— but I have never witnessed such cleverness as you three possess."

Miss Bunsen removed her glasses and looked solemnly at the girls. Well, as solemnly as she could while Brains was trying to jump onto her lap.

"This school has its money troubles, girls, but things are far worse than any of you know. We are deeply in debt. If we win this competition, which we simply must, the money would only

be just enough to pay off all the debts. You see, the school is not just in danger of being closed for repairs. If we do not win this competition, I will have to sell the school to pay our creditors. Miss Bunsen's School for Brilliant Girls will close forever."

The girls looked at one another, horrified. Millie shivered, and even Halinka looked shaken.

"Debts?" Pearl asked.

"Many, unfortunately. There is the company that deals with the woodworm, and there is a lot of woodworm in a building this old. Then there is the builder who has propped up the walls, the carpenter who strengthened the assembly floor to prevent it from collapsing, and the roofer who replaced the tiles above the classrooms to keep my girls dry."

A large drop of water plopped into Miss Bunsen's tea.

"Alas, the budget would not stretch to water-proofing my office."

Pearl looked at Halinka and Millie, knowing exactly what they were thinking. There was no way they could let the school close.

"Girls, you are our only shot at keeping the school open. We must win this competition. That is why I have granted you special permission to stay after school hours tonight and use any of the facilities you would like. I only ask that you take care of Brains. His bladder isn't as strong as it was, and he's prone to fits of coughing, which can lead to other issues, but he could prove useful." Miss Bunsen ran a hand over her bionic cat. "He is a very intelligent cat. I'm quite sure he will aid you in your mission."

Brains coughed up a fur ball and lazily blinked his glass eye.

Millie raised a shaky hand. "What about our

parents, Miss Bunsen? They'll worry if we don't come home."

"I'll let your parents know you'll be here with Mr. Bell. You'll be perfectly safe. I'm counting on you girls. The whole school's future relies on us winning this competition. Now go forth and invent!"

Eyeing each other nervously, Pearl, Halinka, and Millie stood up and left Miss Bunsen's office with Brains trailing behind, his back wheels squeaking.

Brains

Chapter 5

"I don't know about you two, but I need some fresh air and a booster snack after that meeting," Halinka said, pulling her lunch box out of her bag and pushing open the creaky, old wooden doors that led to the yard.

Pearl and Millie smirked. Halinka never could work on an empty stomach. They sat down under an ancient oak tree and gazed up at its rusty-colored leaves.

"I wonder how old this tree is," Millie said, her brow furrowed against the dappled sunlight.

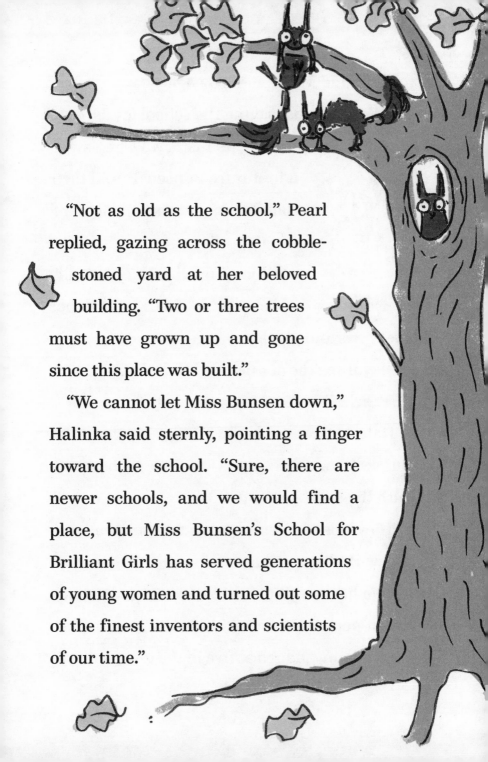

"Not as old as the school," Pearl replied, gazing across the cobble-stoned yard at her beloved building. "Two or three trees must have grown up and gone since this place was built."

"We cannot let Miss Bunsen down," Halinka said sternly, pointing a finger toward the school. "Sure, there are newer schools, and we would find a place, but Miss Bunsen's School for Brilliant Girls has served generations of young women and turned out some of the finest inventors and scientists of our time."

Pearl and Millie nodded eagerly.

"We're not just saving the school for us, or to

preserve its history. We're saving it for future Bunseners and their daughters, and their daughters' daughters."

Millie clapped enthusiastically at Halinka's speech, while Pearl raised her eyebrows and giggled.

"I can see the statue now! Halinka Harrison: The Girl Who Saved Miss Bunsen's."

Halinka lowered her arm. "But it's true. Miss Bunsen's must be saved, and we've been set with the task of saving it!"

They looked solemnly at each other, realizing the work that lay ahead.

"We have until tomorrow evening to get our hat in perfect order," said Pearl. "The competition is being judged at five in the town hall. We can do this."

Millie nervously pulled on her braid. "I think—"

"Hey," Halinka interrupted, pointing at the school gates. "Look who it is."

"Hey, Pearl!" Alima shouted from behind the railing.

Pearl, Halinka, and Millie walked over to the gates where Alima was standing—unfortunately with Megan and Heather in tow.

"It's good to keep bumping into you like this. I'm glad our schools are so close," said Pearl. "How is your invention going for the competition?"

"Well, we haven't actually agreed on an idea yet," Alima said, looking secretly over her shoulder at Megan and Heather. "I wanted to put forward my Grrl Bot idea. It's a robotic friend who can help you with anything, from homework to friend advice." Alima handed

Pearl her sketchbook.

"Hey, I love these robots you've designed," Pearl said, running her hand over the beautifully drawn designs. "And you could certainly use some friend advice!"

Alima giggled. "You're not wrong there! I've got a whole sketchbook of these Grrl Bots and lots of other inventions at home. You should come over and have a look one day."

"I'd like that a lot," Pearl said. "I've missed hanging out with you."

"What are you doing, Alima?" Megan cried, snatching the notebook from Pearl's fingers. "Are you talking about your stupid Grrl Bots again? They are never going to win any prizes. We're going with my and Heather's idea, remember?"

"Get a move on, would you? We need to go into town to buy a few fabulous supplies for our winning invention," Heather said, brandishing a shiny gold credit card.

"Like we even need to bother getting new supplies, with schools like yours in the mix," Heather said, sighing.

"Well, good luck," Pearl said, ignoring them. "I guess we'll see you there tomorrow. Our invention was chosen, by the way."

"That's so exciting! Good luck, guys," Alima called over her shoulder as Heather and Megan dragged her off. "See you tomorrow."

As soon as they were out of earshot, Millie cried, "Oh, *sprockets*! We are never going to win! Did you see that gold card? They will be able to buy anything they want to build their invention, and what do we have? Nothing, apart from a load of junk and an old cat!"

Brains looked up at them through his glass eye. A puddle formed underneath him, slowly edging toward the girls' feet.

"He's sizzling," Halinka said, looking down in disgust. "He shouldn't be sizzling, should he?"

"I think he's just short-circuited his waterworks," Pearl said, peering cautious-ly underneath Brains's tail before turning back toward her friends.

"Look, ladies. We may have no scooters, no gold card, a load of old junk, and a cat that smells of wee, but we can do this! The Atom girls can't even agree on a design to put forward, and by the sounds of it, they haven't even started! Our invention works because of its simplicity and its genius design and our teamwork. It is truly something every child can use. We just need to finesse the tricky bits, and that isn't going to happen while we stand here in a puddle of cat wee, whining about all the things we don't have. Now let's get going!"

"Yeah!" Halinka said, punching the air.

"Okay," murmured Millie, pushing her glasses back up her nose and straightening her braids. "Let's do this."

Chapter 6

Pearl flung open the doors of Miss Bunsen's School for Brilliant Girls and marched inside, her two friends following in close pursuit.

"Halinka," Pearl said firmly, "I need you to go to the sewing room and fetch three yards of fabric."

"There's no fabric left," Millie said. "Miss Bunsen used it to create last summer's fashion line—the one that was going to be sold in all the major stores and make a heap of money for the school."

"What fashion line?" Halinka asked.

"Exactly," Millie said. "Brains drank a whole pot of Miss Bunsen's dandelion tea and had a major accident all over the garments right before they were going to be sold."

Pearl closed her eyes and tried to remain calm.

"Fine," she said. "Halinka, I need you to go to the sewing room and remove the curtains from the windows. We also need a sewing machine, ten bobbins, thread, scissors, zippers, snaps, and anything else you can find. Bring them to the basement under the auditorium. I know Mr. Bell keeps all sorts of useful stuff down there, plus it's quiet and we won't be disturbed."

"On my way," Halinka said, pulling her sunglasses over her eyes and running off down the corridor.

"Millie," Pearl continued, "I need you to collect any old circuit boards you can find.

There's a heap of old computers by the stairs leading up to Miss Bunsen's office. Open those up, and bring all the bits inside, plus any pliers, wire strippers, screws, nuts, and bolts that you can lay your hands on."

"Got it," Millie said, making a note of Pearl's list on the back of her hand.

"I'm going to the library and media room to get some stuff. And Millie…" Pearl said, putting a reassuring hand on her friend's shoulder. "We've got this. Don't worry."

"I know," Millie said, smiling cautiously. "I trust you, Pearl."

Chapter 7

Pearl edged slowly down the basement steps, leaning against the wall to steady herself. She reached into the pitch black, trying to find the light.

"Got it," she whispered, feeling the cord between her fingers and giving it a tug.

"Wow," she gasped as she descended the last few steps and plopped her box of stuff on the workbench in the middle of the large space. "Mr. Bell sure does like his science!"

She gazed all around her at the tidy shelves

full of beakers, measuring jugs, racks of test tubes, and jars of colorful powders and chemicals.

"Whoops!" A loud clatter came from the steps. "Sorry, it's only me," Millie said, fumbling around on the floor for her glasses. "Here, I got the bits."

"Thanks, Millie." Pearl smiled.

"Here I am, never fear! We're good to win this thing!" Halinka stomped down the steps carrying a box with a large pile of ugly, flowery fabric and a sewing machine balanced on top.

"I don't remember the sewing-room curtains being that ugly," Millie said.

"Oh, the sewing-room curtains were even uglier. I got these bad boys from Professor Gilgamesh's archaeology lecture hall."

"Wow," Pearl said quietly, unable to believe that such curtains had ever been chosen for

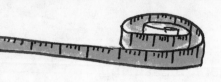

any room. She shook herself back to
the real matter at hand.

"Okay, so let's see what we've got
here."

Pearl laid out all the supplies on the
workbench and hung her design up on
the wall under a bare light bulb.

Before long, the basement was abuzz with
activity. Halinka leaned over her sewing machine, turning the curtains into the
main body of the hat.

"I know that purple thread
doesn't exactly go with the
yellow fabric." She sighed. "But
it's the only spool of thread that
hadn't been chewed to slobbery bits
by Brains."

The cat looked up from the

pile of scraps he was lying on top
of. A yellow thread hung from his
crooked teeth.

"What is that smell?" Millie asked
as she sniffed her soldering iron. "I hope
it's not my circuit boards, or else I've done
something very wrong."

"I don't think it's you," Pearl said,
holding her nose with one hand and
removing something from underneath Brains's bottom with a
tissue in the other.

"Brains!" Halinka cried. "You're
supposed to be *helping*."

Brains flicked his
glass eye toward her,
unashamed.

Suddenly, basement

69

lights flickered. Everyone paused.

"What's going on?" Millie whispered. "I'm scared."

"Maybe Miss Bunsen didn't pay the electricity bill this month." Halinka shrugged, gripping the sewing machine a little tighter than before.

"Brains?" Pearl asked, looking at the cat suspiciously.

There was a knock at the window. The three friends moved closer to one another, squinting to see what was making the noise. Suddenly—BAM—the dusty basement window flipped open, and in flew at least a dozen tiny, winged robots wearing party dresses. They lined up in rows on the workbench, folded their arms, and tilted their heads to one side.

"Alima's Grrl Bots!" Pearl blurted out before stepping in front of her two friends. "Heather and Megan must have decided to go with Alima's design. How can we help you?"

The back row began beatboxing a rhythm and swaying along in time. Then the front Grrl Bots stepped forward and rapped:

Yo, we're the grrls from Atom Academy,
and you can't compete, nah.
We came to eye your sad design,
and we're gonna beat ya, beat ya.

All twelve Grrl Bots flicked their hair one by one and marched back to the open window, though the last was too slow and got caught in Brains's mess. She sizzled and fell over.

The three friends stood in stunned silence, then Halinka spoke up. "Who says 'yo' anymore?

That's so last century."

Millie snorted before composing herself, but Pearl looked concerned.

"You know what this means, don't you?" Pearl said, picking up the broken Grrl Bot.

"The girls at Atom Academy can't rap?" Halinka suggested.

"No," Pearl said, pulling off the Grrl Bot's hair and revealing a camera. "It means that Megan and Heather have used Alima's design to spy on us. I bet each of those Grrl Bots is fitted with a camera. Atom now knows exactly what we're making, so we need to figure out what they're up to."

"They could steal our design!" Millie gasped.

"Do you think Alima is in on it?" Halinka asked.

"I'm not sure," Pearl said. "Anyone fancy a trip up to Atom Academy to see what's going on?"

Chapter 8

By the time Pearl, Halinka, and Millie climbed out of the basement, it was late in the afternoon. The corridors were filled with girls grabbing books from lockers and warm, woolen duffle coats from pegs, rushing out the doors and into the low autumn sun.

"Goodness," said Millie. "We were down in that basement for longer than I thought."

"Too long," Halinka retorted, before realizing she might have sounded a bit moany. "I mean, too long with nothing to snack on!" She headed for the vending machine, its wire coils filled with every exotic fruit imaginable.

"Dragon fruit, anyone?"

"I'm happy with an apple," said Millie, catching the McIntosh Halinka threw.

"Boring," Halinka sniffed, biting into her scaly snack. "Hey, Pearl, are you alright? Fancy a papaya?"

"I'm okay," Pearl replied, "but there is something bothering me a little. Those Grrl Bots were definitely Alima's design. I saw her sketches this afternoon. How could she let Heather and Megan use them against us?"

"Well, Megan and Heather aren't exactly a good influence," Halinka said. "At Atom Academy, you eventually become an Atom girl and forget who you really are."

"Maybe she just doesn't have the confidence to speak up for herself," said Millie, slipping a reassuring arm around Pearl.

"I'm not sure," Pearl said  softly. "What if she's decided she likes Heather and Megan better than me and doesn't want to be friends anymore?"

"Well, her loss!" Halinka barked, slapping Pearl on the back three times in her usual way of showing affection without being all slushy. "Now come on, ladies, we have a school to snoop on!" Halinka pulled her toolbox out of her locker, which was conveniently situated next to the fruit snack machine. "Spying will make you feel better, Pearl."

"Haven't we forgotten someone?" Millie asked. She strapped a baby carrier she had sewn from some leftover curtain fabric to her chest and reached into her locker.

"Sorry, Brains," Pearl said, watching her

friend struggle to fit arms, wheels, and a tail into the canvas pouch.

The girls grabbed their coats and left the building just as the sun was setting behind the hill that led up to Atom Academy.

"We should walk," Pearl said, eyeing their unique vehicles. "We need to attract as little attention as possible."

"She has a cat strapped to her chest!"

"Pearl said 'as little attention *as possible.*'" Millie ignored Halinka and headed toward the rival school. "But please try to be quiet, Brains," she whispered.

They trudged up the hill in silence, watching the town around them. Inside the quiet homes, people were sitting down to dinner, and all along the street, shops closed their shutters and streetlights flickered to life. It seemed far too normal for the sneaking and spying they

were about to do.

Ten minutes later, they'd reached the enormous cuboid building that was Atom Academy. The walls gleamed white in the early moonlight, and the buzz of the school's electric fence drowned out all other sound.

Millie pulled a pair of rubber gloves out of her pocket, along with a screwdriver and a pair of snippers.

"Are you sure you know what you're doing?" Halinka asked, nervously watching her friend crouch down and open the white fuse box by the front gate.

"Shhh!" Millie whispered. "Keep a lookout."

Pearl and Halinka pulled their dark coats over their ears and covered all but their eyes with their scarves. They turned back-to-back and watched the area around them.

"Done," Millie said as she disabled the electric current. The buzzing ceased, and everything was quiet except for the swishing of the gate as it slipped open.

The girls crept around the side of the building where a blue glow was illuminating a solitary window.

"That must be the room where Megan, Heather, and Alima are working. I guess they're working late too." Pearl said, craning her neck up. "What have you got in your bag of tricks, Halinka?"

Halinka was starting to rummage in her toolbox when a howl made her freeze. She turned just in time to see three enormous guard dogs running toward them, teeth bared.

Pearl gasped. "Dogs! Quick, Halinka, you're our squirrel fighter. *Do something!*"

"*Squirrels* are no problem! But I forgot to pack my guard-dog-fending-off machine." Halinka turned to run.

"Good thing I remembered mine," Millie said with a wry smile. With a flourish, she pulled out an impressive gadget loaded with dog

biscuits. "Excuse me, Brains," she said, aiming the machine to the sky.

BAM, BAM, BAM and BAM, BAM, BAM.

The growls turned to excited yelps as the delicious dog biscuits shot off into the distance, the dogs following them in quick pursuit.

"They're organic," Millie said as the dogs disappeared. "And biodegradable."

"I wasn't really worried about that right now," said Halinka. She leaned against the building and clutched at her heart, then dove back into her toolbox. "Okay, girls, get these on your paws!" Halinka pulled out three pairs of glitter boots and gloves.

"What do these do?" asked Pearl.

"They'll help us climb the wall, silly!" said Halinka. "According to my calculations, the glitter will give us extra traction."

A creak from above made the girls back up

81

close to the school wall. Soon, a voice called out the window. "What's going on down there?"

"Urgh, Megan." Halinka shuddered.

"Everyone, quiet," Pearl whispered. She tried to hold her breath.

Brains let out a little cat burp.

"What's going on?" a second, fainter voice hollered from inside.

"Nothing, Heather. Why don't you just get Alima back to copying that hat circuitry and stop being so nosy."

The window slammed shut, and Pearl, Halinka, and Millie all looked at one another, thinking the same thing. They had been right. Atom Academy had stolen their design.

"Well, that proves it," Millie said. "Can we go now? We can tell the judges in the morning."

"Not without proper proof," said Pearl. "We need to know exactly what they're up to."

"Yeah, and I've been waiting for the perfect opportunity to test out these boots and gloves!" Halinka added.

"You mean you've not tested them yet?" Millie asked, trembling slightly.

"Well, I've not tested them as such, but I'm sure they'll be fine."

"We'll just have to trust you, Halinka. Especially as it seems we're out of dog biscuits," Pearl said.

Gingerly, Halinka placed one foot on the wall of Atom Academy, then one hand. "It sticks," she said, and nodded to Pearl and Millie, who began to follow her up the wall. They didn't speak again until they were six feet off the ground.

"They work!" Millie whispered.

"Well, of course they do. I'm a genius," Halinka replied.

They poked their heads over the windowsill and peeked inside. Heather and Megan were painting their nails and drinking pink smoothies through twisty straws, their feet resting on the workbench.

"They don't seem to be doing much," Millie said, adjusting her glasses for a better view.

"Looks like Alima is the chief copycat here," Halinka said.

"I just can't believe that Alima would betray me like this," Pearl said.

But sure enough, Alima was huddled over a workbench with a spread of photographs showing the Bunsen girls' hat and all the design drawings, obviously taken by the Grrl Bots. In front of her was a hat that looked very similar to theirs, but instead of being made from ugly curtain fabric, this hat was sewn with shiny pink silk, and all the pieces were made from brand-new materials. It was the Bunsen girls' hat for sure, just shinier.

Millie stretched out one of the toggles on her duffle coat and took some pictures with the camera hidden inside, then pulled a listening device out of her pocket and stuck it to the window.

"Oh, blow my light bulbs! It won't stick."

"Here," Halinka said, presenting Millie with a lump of freshly chewed bubble gum.

"Thanks," Millie said unconvincingly as she took the lump and popped it on the window.

"Perfect!" Halinka exclaimed, looking pleased with herself.

"Shh! Listen," Pearl whispered, holding an earpiece close to her and her friends. "What are they saying?"

"So, what are we going to spend our prize money on when this stupid hat wins the competition?" Heather asked Megan breezily. "I think the school swimming pool could use new tiles. That seahorse pattern is *so* last year."

"I know!" Megan replied, snorting. "Who has seahorse tiles in their pool these days? It's totally all about sea turtles now."

"I don't get why this hat is such a big deal anyway," Alima said. "We had a plan. We were going to enter my Grrl Bots in the competition."

"We only built the Grrl Bots to spy, Alima. Duh! Even Miss Acid knew that," Megan said.

"But we don't even need to win this prize money! Atom has more money than it knows what to do with."

"Because the Bunsen girls come up with the best ideas, and we can't let them seem smarter than us," Heather snapped. "*And* they

only have scraps to make them with, and their headmistress is as mad as a box of frogs. Do you really want to be beaten in a competition by a bunch of crazy girls who have a dump of a school that's barely even standing?"

"Heather is right, Alima. If they win the cash, they'll soon have all the best equipment. *We* are the best school, and things need to stay that way. Get it?"

"But I don't want to cheat," Alima said. "My Grrl Bots—"

There was a loud snap, and then bits of broken Grrl Bot clattered to the floor. *"Finish the hat,"* Megan hissed. Pearl gasped.

Megan glanced out the window at the sound, and the Bunseners ducked so fast they nearly fell off the wall.

"I think we should get going now, before we get caught," Millie said, removing the listening device and popping it back in her pocket.

"What's that smell?" Pearl asked as she began to edge down the facade of the building. Brains was looking decidedly fretful.

"Why is his glass eye bulging like that?" Halinka asked, leaning away.

With a very loud *POP*, Brains's mechanical glass eye shot out of its socket and embedded itself in the glass window above, making a very large crack.

"Quick!" Pearl said. "Down, down, down!"

"If you tap your gloves together, you'll go into a controlled slide," said Halinka.

Pearl, Halinka, and Millie slid down the building. They tiptoed around the dogs before breaking for the exit as fast as they could.

"Do you think we made it?" asked Millie. "If we get caught, will it be a police matter, do you think?"

"It had better be!" said Halinka, panting. "*They* stole from *us*, after all! Let's have them arrested!"

"Just hope they didn't see us," said Pearl. "We've got a hat to finish." She risked a look back at Atom Academy over her shoulder and crossed her fingers that they had vanished into the night.

Chapter 9

Halinka stretched her arms above her head and yawned widely. "Who knew a basement floor could be so comfy!"

"Well, it's news to me," Millie croaked as she fumbled about for her glasses and started to twiddle with her braids. "I was kept awake all night by squirrels."

Pearl opened a packet of cookies and passed them around. "You could sleep anywhere, Halinka!"

Millie took a cookie and moved

closer to Pearl.

"Are you okay? I mean with what we saw last night, you must be shocked to discover that Alima is involved in stealing our idea."

"Why don't you just keep mentioning it, Millie!" Halinka butted in. "I'm sure Pearl really needs you to remind her."

Millie blushed and fiddled with her braids more intensely.

"Oh, it's okay, Millie," Pearl said, putting her arm around Millie. "At least she didn't sound happy about it. I'm worried about what she's gotten herself into."

"Well, Alima and her two plastic fantastic friends have landed us in it, and the school!" Halinka snapped back. "They stole our invention!"

"But we have photos to prove they copied us," Pearl said.

"Not anymore," Millie replied as she pulled her coat out from underneath sleeping Brains. "It seems Brains had a little accident in the night, and the camera is ruined."

Pearl and Halinka wrinkled their noses in disgust.

"Can someone remind me why this cat is here?" Halinka muttered to herself, spraying a little perfume in Brains's direction.

"We can just tell Miss Bunsen that Atom stole our idea!" Millie chirped enthusiastically. "Then they will be disqualified."

Pearl sighed. "Millie, even if Miss Bunsen believes us, no one else will. We'll just get in trouble for trespassing on Atom's property."

"But the whole school saw our design. We'll

have backup," Millie added, trying to remain hopeful.

"You heard what Heather said. No one from Miss Bunsen's will *ever* be believed over someone from Atom Academy. Especially not Miss Bunsen. They'll think *we* copied Atom."

Millie stared at the floor, blinking back tears. Unexpectedly, Halinka was the first to rally her.

"Hat or no hat, we still need to win this thing. So, we need a plan." Halinka jumped to her feet. "Anyone got any ideas?"

"Yes, I do," said Pearl. "I've been awake all night thinking about this."

Pearl handed Millie a notebook filled with sketches. "Can you get that broken Grrl Bot working again?"

Millie nodded.

"Halinka," Pearl continued, "I need this Grrl Bot fitted with a remote-control mechanism.

Have you got the bits to do that?"

"I can certainly find them!" Halinka replied, pulling a piece of bubble gum out from under the workbench.

"So this is the plan: we fix up the Grrl Bot and fly her back to Atom using the remote control. We take photos of Alima's workstation with the Grrl Bot's camera, which should give us the proof we need."

"Oh, that's brilliant!" Millie squealed in delight. "Do you think she could pick up Brains's missing eye while she's at it? It's probably still stuck in the window!"

"Ha!" Halinka laughed. "Perfect! We'll show those cheaters, and our hat will be the winner!"

A knock at the basement door interrupted her, and Miss Bunsen swooped in.

"Good morning, girls," she gushed as several squirrels

scampered out from underneath her flowing black cloak. "I've come to check on your progress. You've got nine hours to go! You know we're all rooting for you. Can I see the hat?"

"Well, there has been a slight—" Millie began before Halinka elbowed her in the ribs.

"Everything's...fine," Pearl managed to mutter, holding her notebook behind her back. "Here you go, Miss Bunsen! It's coming along!"

Miss Bunsen smiled as she tried on the hat. "It's a shame you had to use those terrible curtains," she said, and flipped the switch on the hat. After a moment, she exclaimed. "Oooh, you know, with your hat on, I don't mind the fabric so much! I'm feeling more confident already!"

"Just as you should," said Pearl, taking back the invention. "Everything is shipshape."

"Well," Miss Bunsen said, turning on her heels and heading back up the basement steps. "I'll leave you three geniuses to it. I don't want to disturb the magic!"

Pearl waited some moments until after Miss Bunsen had closed the basement door. "I don't know how we'll win. We'll think of something. Right now, the first priority is to stop Atom."

Halinka and Millie nodded grimly, and each got to work on the Grrl Bot. After several hours of tinkering, the three brilliant Bunsen girls opened the basement window and guided the bot off on her mission.

Millie flicked on a small monitor, and the three girls watched as the Grrl Bot flew into Atom Academy through an open window and landed on the workbench where the hat was sitting.

"Where are they?" Halinka asked, staring at the grainy picture.

"Luckily for us, they're not there!" Pearl sighed.

Millie took a few photographs of the room and then guided the Grrl Bot back to the window to pick up the missing eye. "Done," she said, and the Grrl Bot began her journey back down the hill.

"Mission accomplished," Pearl cried. "Now we just have to hope our hat works perfectly and those Atom girls get their just deserts." She high-fived Halinka.

"Um, Pearl," said Millie, who was still flying the Grrl Bot.

"Yes, Millie?"

"I think we have company." Millie pointed

to her screen. Where there had been blue sky, there were now dozens of Grrl Bots.

The screen went black, and the Bunsen girls ran out the door.

Halfway up the hill to Atom, they found the Grrl Bot, destroyed by her sisters. Millie opened a compartment. "At least Brains's eye survived," she said.

"Yeah, but did the camera?" asked Halinka. "We need proof!"

Millie shook her head.

Pearl sighed. "We'll have to figure something out. It's almost time." But secretly, Pearl was worried about the judges. With two identical hats entered, wouldn't everyone assume that Miss Bunsen's School was the copycat?

Chapter 10

Pearl, Halinka, and Millie lifted their hat onto the stand labeled "Miss Bunsen's School for Brilliant Girls" and looked around them at all the other inventions. There was a self-cleaning rabbit hutch from Cogs College, with built-in functions for grooming and trimming bunny claws; an unfillable, bottomless school bag from Hadron High that never got heavy, no matter how many books or

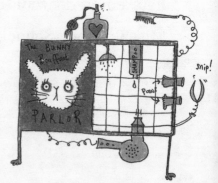

stale sandwiches were left inside; a special spicy sauce from the School of Culinary Science that made even the most disgusting boiled cabbage taste delicious; and, of course, the hat from Atom Academy.

Miss Acid, the head of Atom Academy, stood beside it, arguing with Miss Bunsen.

"Miss Bunsen," the girls overheard, "I can assure you that my girls would never copy an idea. It must be a coincidence that your girls' invention is similar to ours. Though I believe Atom's entry is a bit more...professional." She sniffed.

"Why does it matter what the hat *looks* like?" asked Millie. "The confidence it gives you should make you not care what others think!"

"Look who's here," Halinka scoffed, folding her arms and leaning up against the stand.

"Oh, what a darling little invention," Megan said to Pearl as she and Heather walked past. Alima followed closely behind, red-eyed, her gaze on the floor.

"Oh, sir!" Megan hollered over her shoulder to a stern-looking man holding a clipboard. "These are the three you're looking for."

Pearl, Halinka, and Millie were swarmed by several important-looking people with clipboards and frowns. The frowniest of all was Professor Petrinsky.

One of the judges looked at them crossly as Miss Bunsen hurried over. "We've just had word that these three girls were caught trespassing on Atom Academy's property last night. I've reviewed the tapes, and you three were definitely up to something."

"Girls," Miss Bunsen said, her eyes watery behind her half-moon glasses. "Is this true?"

The three friends looked at one another, unsure what to say.

Professor Petrinsky stepped forward.

"I'm very, very disappointed to hear this," he said, scratching his bald patch. "And moreover, I'm very surprised. Bunsen girls never cheat. Breaking onto another school's campus is serious. I'm sorry to say that I have no choice but to disqualify Miss Bunsen's School for Brilliant Girls from the competition."

"There's a proper explanation—" Halinka said, but before she could finish, one of the judges removed their hat from its stand. Miss Bunsen burst into tears. Millie moved to comfort her, but Penelope, the head girl, elbowed her out of the way.

Miss Bunsen and Penelope whispered together, then Penelope grabbed Halinka and Pearl by the arm and marched them out of the room. Millie had no choice but to follow. Penelope only slowed down to pick up Brains, who was meowing at her feet.

"I've been given strict instructions to keep you in the basement until further notice," she said. "What were you thinking? We were depending on you! I've never seen Miss Bunsen so upset."

"But—" said Millie, meekly.

"I don't want to hear it," snapped Penelope. "You let me down. You let us *all* down. This will take some getting over, if we ever get over it. The school will close. Where are we supposed to *go*?"

Pearl didn't even try to protest. It was just as she had warned this morning. Why hadn't they realized that a school willing to cheat would turn them in for spying? Why hadn't they thought there would be security cameras?

They shuffled into the town hall's musty basement and sat down. Pearl eyed the piles of holiday decorations and old banners. If only they could have built their hat out of those instead of the terrible curtains!

Penelope positioned herself on the basement steps and opened up a thick copy of *Terrific Turbines*. "No talking," she growled.

"Oh, I have that book," Millie said. "I love chapter four."

Pearl looked sadly at Brains. "I guess we let you down too. Sorry, buddy." Brains turned his head and blinked at her—with only one eye, of course. Pearl hadn't had a chance to give him back the eye they'd rescued from Atom.

"Wait!" Pearl whispered. *"That's it!* Don't you remember? Brains's glass eye is a camera!

That's how Miss Bunsen knew we were at her office door!"

"Quiet!" shouted Penelope. "This is meant to be a punishment."

"Yes," Halinka said, ignoring the head girl. "That means Brains's eye would have recorded everything that went on in that room after we left."

"Brilliant!" Millie said. "Can you toss it to me? I can probably rig it up to work as a projector."

They glanced at Penelope, who was staring at them furiously. "This is *detention*," she began. "It is *not*—"

"Over to you, Brains," whispered Pearl.

Brains let out an enormous blast of wind from his bottom, then coughed several hair balls covered

109

in mackerel cat food onto Penelope's shoes. Penelope jumped up and desperately tried to wipe off the mess.

"I'll be right back," she whimpered and gave Brains a dirty look. *Do not move.*

"Oh, well done, Brains," Pearl said, scratching him behind the ears. She waited for Penelope to get safely away from the door and then tossed the eye to Millie.

"I can get this working, no problem," Millie said, pulling some copper wire and a screwdriver out of her pocket.

"And—excellent! It looks like the images are stored in the eye. Halinka, can you scavenge a fiber-optic LED bit from anything down here? The lens is a crystal, so that should work!"

Pearl and Halinka studied the mess in the basement. In the corner was a heap of old computers that they had pulled apart in no time. After a few minutes of fiddling, Millie had fixed the eye—and luckily, Penelope had not returned.

"Come on, girls." Pearl beamed happily. "Let's get upstairs and show everyone what's really going on."

Chapter 11

The town hall was silent as the three friends crept in the back door and hid behind the umbrella rack. The Atom girls were beginning their demonstration. Miss Bunsen stood to the side of the audience, sniffling into a very old handkerchief.

"Poor Miss Bunsen," Millie said. "She must think we're terrible."

Onstage, Megan wore the shiny hat, while Heather and Alima stood on either side.

"Phew." Halinka sighed. "There's still time.

Quick, we need to get that video running!"

Halinka and Millie kept watching from behind the umbrella stand, while Pearl snuck around behind all the chairs toward where Miss Bunsen and Professor Petrinsky were standing.

"Pearl Peppersmith!" Miss Bunsen was shocked to see one of her girls disobeying her. "You had better have a very good explanation for not being in detention!"

"I do," Pearl said. "Professor Petrinsky, I have some very important evidence—" But the professor ignored her and continued watching the Atom girls onstage.

"See how our incredible Best of Yourself Hat helps your vocabulary in any conversation," Heather announced. "Megan, how are you today? Are you well?"

Megan flicked a tiny, silver switch on the hat's brim. "I'm in fine fettle, my darling Heather. In fact, I'm feeling as fine and fluffy as a fluffy squirrel's tail. And yourself?"

The town hall erupted into applause. Beside Pearl, Professor Petrinsky looked very impressed.

"Next I shall demonstrate our hat's incredible ability to give even a pointless person a boost of confidence. Our classmate Alima is the perfect person to demonstrate this function."

Heather yanked the hat from Megan's head, pushed Alima to the front of the stage, and roughly pulled the hat over Alima's sleek black hair. She looked like a squirrel in the headlights, all eyes on her.

"Flick the switch, dummy," Heather told Alima as she reached over and flipped a diamond-encrusted switch on the hat. Alima's expression began to change.

While Alima paused, Pearl seized her chance. "Professor Petrinsky, we have some important information to show you." She hit a button on Brains's mechanical eye, and a projection appeared behind the Atom girls. A black-and-white image of the Atom Academy classroom where Heather, Megan, and Alima had been working appeared on the back wall behind the stage. Audio played too—crackling, but clear enough to hear that Heather and Megan had forced Alima to steal the Bunsen design.

"WHAT is going on?" Megan cried.

"What is the meaning of this?" asked Professor Petrinsky, storming up onto the stage. "Who invented this hat?"

"We did," said Heather, trying to cover up the image. "This video is *clearly* doctored."

Pearl looked at Alima.

"I built the hat," Alima said quietly. The hall gasped. Halinka and Millie protested, but Pearl was defeated. She turned off the projection. If Alima wouldn't back her up, what hope did she have?

"I built the hat," Alima said again, clearer and stronger, "but I built it from designs stolen from Miss Bunsen's School. I didn't want to. But I didn't have the confidence to stand up for myself until I wore the Best of Yourself Hat. It truly is a great invention."

"It was Pearl's design," Millie said.

"But Millie did the circuits, and Halinka sewed it," Pearl said quickly, before running up to the stage and taking Alima by the hand. "And Alima saved it."

There was silence as Professor Petrinsky considered the two girls. "It appears we were

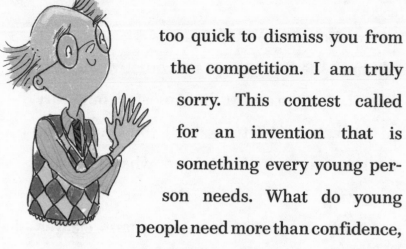

too quick to dismiss you from the competition. I am truly sorry. This contest called for an invention that is something every young person needs. What do young people need more than confidence, honesty, and truthful, loyal friendships? All demonstrated perfectly by the invention I have chosen. I therefore declare that the winner of my competition is Miss Bunsen's School for Brilliant Girls and their Best of Yourself Hat!"

The town hall erupted into cheers, with hats, scarves, and squirrels flying into the air.

Pearl hugged Alima. "Thank you!" she cried.

Alima smiled at her. "I'm sorry it took me so long to do what's right," she said. "I never wanted to betray you."

"Don't worry," Halinka said, racing up to

118

them. "This softy trusted
you the whole time."

The three Bunseners
stood proudly on the
stage beside their friend.
Miss Bunsen came up to
join them, but she was crying
so hard, she couldn't hold the trophy.

After Pearl, Millie, and Halinka had shaken
many hands—and accepted many apologies
from the contest organizers—they found Miss
Bunsen in the hallway, Brains at her side. "My
brilliant girls," she said. "I am so very proud of
you. You've saved our school!"

Pearl knelt down next to Brains and popped his
glass eye back in. "You were right, Miss Bunsen.
We couldn't have done this without Brains!"

"He is a very special cat," said Miss Bunsen.
"And a rather troublesome one sometimes. But

enough! It's time for you three to celebrate and then get some rest. School still starts at nine tomorrow, and even geniuses need to sleep! Have you three seen Alima? I want to see about hiring some of those Grrl Bots for squirrel patrol."

Halinka cheered. "If you need a captain for your squirrel-fighting force, don't forget to call on me, Miss Bunsen," she said.

Pearl, Millie, and Halinka left the town hall, carrying their large trophy between them. In the setting sun, they paused at the gates and looked up at their beloved school.

"Look, Halinka," Pearl said, laughing. "I see a space for your statue! 'Halinka Harrison: The Girl Who Saved Miss Bunsen's.'"

Halinka grinned and put her arms around her friends. "Any statue would have to also have Pearl Peppersmith and Millie Maranova," she said. "The *girls* who saved Miss Bunsen's."

"And Alima!" said Millie. "And Brains! Though maybe he should have both eyes in the statue."

"I'm sure we could design one with a mechanical eye that pops out," Pearl said. "It might be steam-powered."

Halinka laughed. "You know what? That would sure scare all the squirrels!"

100 Years of

Albert Whitman & Company

1919–2019

Albert Whitman & Company encompasses all ages and reading levels, including board books, picture books, early readers, chapter books, middle grade, and YA

Present

2017

The Boxcar Children celebrates its 75th anniversary and the second Boxcar Children movie, *Surprise Island*, is scheduled to be released

The first Boxcar Children movie is released

2014

2008

John Quattrocchi and employee Pat McPartland buy Albert Whitman & Company, continuing the tradition of keeping it independently owned and operated

Losing Uncle Tim, a book about the AIDS crisis, wins the first-ever Lambda Literary Award in the Children's/YA category

1989

1970

The first Albert Whitman issues book, *How Do I Feel?* by Norma Simon, is published

Three states boycott the company after it publishes *Fun for Chris*, a book about integration

1956

1942

The Boxcar Children is published

Pecos Bill: The Greatest Cowboy of All Time wins a Newbery Honor Award

1938

1919

Albert Whitman & Company is started

Albert Whitman begins his career in publishing

Early 1900s

Celebrate with us in 2019!
Find out more at www.albertwhitman.com.